ENCOUNTERS IN END CITY

ENCOUNTERS IN END CITY

MINECRAFTERS ACADEMY

BOOK SIX

Winter Morgan

Sky Pony Press
New York

Copyright © 2017 by Hollan Publishing, Inc.

Minecraft® is a registered trademark of Notch Development AB.

The Minecraft game is copyright © Mojang AB.

Sky Pony Press books may be purchased in bulk at special discounts for sales promotion, corporate gifts, fund-raising, or educational purposes. Special editions can also be created to specifications. For details, contact the Special Sales Department, Sky Pony Press, 307 West 36th Street, 11th Floor, New York, NY 10018 or info@skyhorsepublishing.com.

Sky Pony® is a registered trademark of Skyhorse Publishing, Inc.®, a Delaware corporation.

Minecraft® is a registered trademark of Notch Development AB. The Minecraft game is copyright © Mojang AB.

Visit our website at www.skyponypress.com.

10 9 8 7 6 5 4 3 2 1

Library of Congress Cataloging-in-Publication Data is available on file.

Cover Design by Brian Peterson
Cover photo by Megan Miller

Print ISBN: 978-1-5107-1822-7
Ebook ISBN: 978-1-5107-1831-9

Printed in Canada

TABLE OF CONTENTS

ENCOUNTERS IN END CITY

Chapter 1
GEARING UP FOR GRADUATION

J ulia walked toward the familiar dorm room that she had called home during the past few years at Minecrafters Academy. Recently, every time Julia entered the dorms, she felt sad. Graduation was a short while away, and Julia was dreading it. She loved being at Minecrafters Academy and would miss it. Although she knew that her real life was in the Cold Biome, she was enjoying being a student and spending time with her roommates, Mia and Emma.

Julia entered the room and called out, "Mia, are you ready?"

Mia stood by the closet, filling up a chest with extra supplies from her inventory. "Yes, I'm so excited. I can't believe the farm is completed." Mia closed the chest.

"You worked really hard on the farm." Julia smiled.

"It was all Steve," Mia explained. "He's such a great teacher. Now that I have these new skills, I've contacted a few people who've asked me to build farms for them."

"But when will you find the time?" Julia asked. "We have our schoolwork."

"Julia, you know we only have a short time until this is all over. I start working when school is finished," Mia said. "I'm excited to get back to the real world and start working on farms."

Julia couldn't understand why Mia was so excited to graduate and start a life as a farmer. If Julia had been given the option of extending her time at school, she'd stay at Minecrafters Academy for a few more years. Unlike Mia, Julia was in was no great rush to go out into the Overworld. Yet Julia was happy for her friend Mia. "Wow, that's impressive. I can't believe you already have clients lined up after you leave school."

"They're just small jobs," Mia replied modestly, "but it's a start."

"I have no idea what I'm going to do after graduation," Julia confessed. "In fact, I'm not looking forward to it at all. I'll miss living with you and Emma, and having Cayla down the hall."

Emma walked in and, having overheard them, admitted, "I feel the same way. I'm going to miss you guys. It's been so much fun living with you, and we make a great team."

Cayla sprinted into the room with Brad. "Guys," she said, "we're going to be really late."

"We don't want to disappoint Steve," Brad told them. "I think he wants us to stand next to him as he cuts the ribbon."

Mia looked out the window. "There's already a large crowd standing next to the farm. I think we should hurry."

The group rushed toward the farm and arrived as the opening ceremony was about to begin. Steve called out to the crowd, "I'd like the volunteers to join me as I cut the ribbon."

Mia looked over at Emma. "We made it just in time."

The gang weaved through the crowd, making their way toward Steve. Julia looked at the large red mushrooms that grew from the structure she'd constructed with Brad, and was glad that Mia suggested she volunteer at the farm.

"I'm proud to announce that the school farm is completed. However, this doesn't mean that we won't stop working on it. It does mean that we've yielded crops from our first harvest and we will feast on these treats tonight on the great lawn. Everyone is invited to join us as we share our abundant crops!"

The crowd cheered, but hushed when Steve spoke again. "I have another announcement. I'm sad to say that this is my last year at Minecrafters Academy. I've enjoyed being a visiting teacher, but I must get back to my wheat farm."

Lucy stood next to Steve. "It was great to have you be a part of the Minecrafters Academy community. I hope you come back to join us soon."

Hearing those words, Steve smiled and cut the red ribbon, inviting everyone to view the garden.

Steve asked the volunteers, "Will you stay and help me pick crops from the garden for the feast?"

The gang agreed. After the crowds cleared, they picked potatoes, carrots, apples, and other crops. Emma stood by the mushrooms. "I'm so glad we can finally have mushrooms. I've been craving them ever since we got back from Mushroom Island."

"After school ends, you can come visit me at Mushroom Island," Cayla suggested.

Julia asked, "Can I come too?"

"Yes, everyone is invited," Cayla said. "You've been to my house and you know it has more than enough room for all of my friends."

Julia was happy that her friends at school wanted to keep in contact with her, but she knew once they got back to their old lives, it would be hard to keep in touch.

When the table overflowed with fruit and other crops, Steve signaled that they were done. "I think we have enough. This is going to be an epic feast."

Steve was right. The feast was epic and rather gluttonous. Steve and the staff cooked chicken, beef, cookies, and cakes. Emma walked over to Julia, whose plate was piled high with food. "This is amazing."

Julia swallowed her chicken. "Yes, what a great way to celebrate all of the work we've done for the garden."

Mia and Steve joined them. Steve smiled. "I still can't get over this amazing feast."

Mia called Lucy over and asked, "Can we make this an annual tradition?"

"That's a great idea," Lucy replied.

"Perfect," Mia said. "It's nice to know that people will celebrate the farm when we're no longer students here."

Nick and Jamie walked over to them. Nick asked, "We did a good job, right?"

"The feast is great, but it's not just our work. A lot of people were involved. Also, they're going to make this an annual tradition," Mia said.

"Wow," Jamie exclaimed. "That's so cool."

Julia tried to imagine all the new students dining at the feast, but it was too hard. She looked up at the sky. The sun was starting to set, and she knew the feast would be over soon.

As everyone mingled, Lucy called out, "Before you finish your meal, I have an announcement."

The partygoers walked over to Lucy as she spoke. "As you all know, graduation is approaching. I will be choosing a class speaker who will have the honor of giving a speech at this event. This is a position that means a lot to the school so we will do an extensive search for the speaker who best represents the school's values."

A student asked, "How will you conduct the search?"

Lucy replied, "Good question. There are some competitions that will take place where we will evaluate students."

Julia's stomach started to hurt when she heard Lucy utter the word *competitions*, and she wished she hadn't eaten so much chicken. Julia disliked competition. After all the drama with the Minecrafters Academic Olympics, Julia wasn't in the mood for another contest.

"What type of competitions?" Julia questioned.

"I don't want to go into specifics now, but I will hold an assembly tomorrow morning after breakfast where I will go over everything. That said, in addition to the evaluations, I will also review your overall achievements at Minecrafters Academy and how you work well with others. As you know, working well with others is a huge part of success at this school. If you demonstrate that ability, you will be on the top of my list. I will continue this talk tomorrow," Lucy said and wished everyone a good night.

Students didn't pay attention to the setting sun. They were fixating on the upcoming competition. Lucy's announcement at the end of the meal kept everyone at the feast longer than they should have stayed. Everyone was busy chatting about which student might be chosen for the role of class speaker and everyone lost track of the time until Nick called out, "Watch out!"

A skeleton army marched across the campus, toting bows and arrows.

Chapter 2
PICK ME

Two block-headed skeletons stood inches from Julia. Arrows flew toward her and before she could put on her armor or grab a sword, an arrow sliced through her arm. Julia wailed as she reached into her inventory for her sword, barely grasping the weapon. Another arrow pierced her other arm. Julia fumbled with her sword and it dropped to the ground.

A zombie spawned and lumbered toward the dropped sword. Julia tried to stop the newly spawned beast, knowing that an armed zombie alongside a skeleton attack would be almost impossible to defeat. She made it over to her dropped weapon. With a renewed energy, she slammed her sword against the zombie's rotten flesh, holding her breath to avoid the odor. With three strikes of her sword, she destroyed the zombie and collected the dropped rotten flesh from the ground. Two arrows flew toward her as she ducked and sprinted toward the skeletons. She plunged her sword into the skeleton's bony body with great force, cracking its rattling frame. She hit both skeletons and was confident she'd defeat them until she felt the sting of arrows pelt her back. Julia awoke in her room, calling out for her roommates, but the room was silent.

Julia placed a torch on her wall, raced to the window, and looked out at the campus. It was dark, but she could see three greenish and rather ghoulish creepers sneaking up behind Mia and Emma. She tried to shout for them to turn around, but it was too late. Julia watched as the fiery creatures exploded and destroyed her friends.

"Julia," Emma called out as she spawned in her bed.

"What happened?" asked a confused Mia.

"You were destroyed by creepers," Julia informed her.

Mia sat up. "Should we stay here for the night?"

Emma asked in a sleepy haze, "Maybe we should go out and help everyone?"

A loud voice was heard throughout the campus. "Head back to your rooms until morning. I repeat, everyone stay in your rooms."

"Was that Lucy?" Mia asked.

"I think so," Emma said.

Julia crawled back in the bed, covering herself with a blue blanket, and wished her friends a good night. Of course, getting to sleep wasn't easy. Julia was distracted by the battle outside her window. The roommates were also awakened by alerts telling them hostile mobs were close by, which they decided to ignore due to Lucy's instructions. Even though Lucy had asked the students to head back to the dorms, Julia knew some people were fighting the hostile mobs that crowded on the great lawn. Julia tried to fall asleep. She even counted sheep, but it didn't work. She was wide-awake.

"Do you think this was one of Lucy's tests?" Mia asked.

Julia was glad she wasn't the only one having trouble sleeping. "What do you mean?"

"When Lucy made that important announcement right before dusk, she knew she was putting us in jeopardy. Maybe she wanted to see how we'd handle the battle," Mia said.

"That makes sense," said Emma, who admitted that she couldn't sleep due to the excitement from the battle.

Even if they could have slept, it wouldn't have been for long because, almost instantly, zombies ripped their door from its hinges and down the hall, Cayla screamed for help.

"Zombies!" Emma jumped up from her bed, quickly putting on her armor. The other girls followed Emma, clutching their swords as they rushed toward the door.

A vacant-eyed zombie reeking of fetid-smelling, rotting flesh raised its arms and readied itself for an attack against Julia's roommates. She swung her sword, hitting the zombie, and its flesh oozed out its body. With a second strike she destroyed the zombie, and decided not to pick up the rotten flesh that dropped on the floor. Instead she sprinted toward Cayla's room as her friends battled the remaining zombies. Cayla's cries grew louder as Julia raced down the hall to help her.

The zombies had ripped Cayla's door off the hinges and were surrounding Cayla. An exhausted Cayla struck out at the group of four zombies with her sword, but she was outnumbered and destroyed, only to spawn and fight the same battle all over again. Julia surprised the zombies and struck one with her sword. Cayla had weakened the zombies, making them easier to battle. One by one, Julia slammed her sword into their backs, obliterating them.

"Thanks," Cayla said. "It was so awful. Every time I was destroyed, I'd have to fight the zombies again. I couldn't do it alone."

"Watch out!" Julia cried as two creepers spawned in the open closet behind Cayla. Julia quickly traded in her sword for a bow and arrow and aimed at the creepers, striking each one. They exploded inches from Cayla.

"Wow, you saved me again," Cayla thanked Julia.

"We have to craft a new door quickly." Julia grabbed wood from her inventory and started to build a new door to replace the one that the zombies had destroyed.

Cayla helped Julia construct the door. When it was finished she said, "We make a great team."

"You certainly do," a voice called out from the hall.

Cayla and Julia turned around to find Lucy standing in the hall. Julia was surprised.

"It's time to go to bed," Lucy informed them. "Julia, please head back to your room."

As Julia walked back to her dorm room, she wondered if Mia was correct in thinking this night battle might be a part of the competition for class speaker. If this was a test, did she win?

Chapter 3
TEAM PLAYERS

Julia walked through the cafeteria with her breakfast, and Cayla asked, "Don't you think it was odd that Lucy was outside the room last night?"

"It was strange." Julia picked up a slice of cake from her plate and took a bite. "But I think she was just checking that we were all safe. It makes sense."

"I bet she was watching how we handled our battle with the zombies, and I'm guessing she is considering us for class speaker," Cayla said.

"What?" Mia asked. She had heard Cayla as she approached the table. "You guys are being considered for class speaker?"

"No," Julia said and then reprimanded Cayla. "Cayla, that's how rumors start."

"Last night, Lucy was outside my door and saw Julia and I working together to destroy zombies," Cayla explained.

"That doesn't mean you're going to be class speaker," Emma said.

Julia swallowed another bite of her cake. "I don't want us getting caught up in the competition. Remember the Olympics? I'd hate to jeopardize our friendship over who will be chosen to be class speaker."

"I know," Cayla said, "but I really want to be class speaker."

"Me too," Mia added.

"Same," Emma said.

"What about you?" Cayla looked at Julia.

Julia didn't want to admit that she dreamt about standing in front of the graduating class, telling them about her incredible experience at the school. She didn't want them to know that ever since Lucy mentioned the class speaker, she couldn't think of anything else. Julia was conflicted. She did want it, but she didn't want to compete with her friends. She stood silently until Cayla asked, "Aren't you going to reply?"

"I want to be class speaker. I really do, but I don't want to compete with you guys. If there was a way we could all do it together, I'd be thrilled," Julia told them.

Brad walked over. "You guys are talking about class speaker, aren't you?"

"How could you tell?" Julia smiled.

"Do you want to be the class speaker, Brad?" Mia asked.

"Nope." Brad blushed. "I freeze every time I stand in front of a crowd. I'd be the worst class speaker."

"Well, at least we won't be competing with Brad," Emma said.

Julia took a sip of milk. "I think we should go to the assembly and hear what Lucy has to say about the class speaker job."

As the group walked through the crowded dining hall, the lights went out. Julia quickly grabbed a torch from her inventory as a spider jockey spawned in the dark cafeteria. Its red eyes shined, and the skeleton's arrows ripped through Emma's left shoulder. Another arrow flew through the air and Julia jumped in front of Emma, shielding her from the arrow.

Brad had skillfully suited up in his armor. Sprinting toward the skeleton, he threw the bony beast from the spider's body. Mia raced next to Brad and slayed the eight-legged spider as Brad slammed his sword and a potion on the skeleton. The enemy was destroyed, but the lights were still off, making the students vulnerable to a hostile mob attack.

Julia walked toward the exit with the other students. They wanted to get outside in the daylight, but she was stopped when two block-carrying Endermen silently walked through the cafeteria. One of the block-carrying Endermen locked eyes with Julia and unleashed a high-pitched shriek.

"Julia, run!" Mia screamed.

As the Enderman teleported toward her, Brad rushed to Julia's side, clutching his glass of water. He splashed the water on the Enderman as other students joined in, destroying the lanky Enderman.

Lucy walked into the dining hall as the lights came back on. "I'd like everyone to meet me on the great lawn. I want to have the assembly and talk about the teams in which I'll be placing you."

"Teams?" Julia asked.

"We can be on a team together," Mia said.

"I wonder how many people we can choose," Emma said.

Brad admitted, "I don't want to be on your team. If you guys are chosen to be class speakers, I don't want to be asked to stand in front of the school."

"Brad," Julia said, "you have to learn to get over your fear of public speaking. It's an important skill."

"I've gotten this far in life without public speaking, I think I'll be fine," Brad retorted.

"But maybe I can help you get over it," Julia said.

"I don't want to get over it. Everyone has fears they don't want to deal with, right? I mean, what's yours?" Brad asked Julia.

She pondered this question as she walked out onto the great lawn. Julia was afraid of many things, but now that Brad asked her to name them, her mind drew blank. What she did fear was losing her friends. "I don't like competitions," she confessed.

"Neither do I," Brad said.

Lucy called the students onto the great lawn and addressed the group. "I wish I could choose everyone to be a class speaker, but I am following a tradition at Minecrafters Academy. This tradition gives one person the honor of speaking during the graduation.

"We will be considering students who have not only demonstrated the skills they've learned while attending the school, but those who understand the importance of working together as a group. After we break you into teams you will work with your team over the next few weeks on various challenges. The faculty will evaluate your individual skill, strategy, and ability to work with others."

The students stood in silence. Julia's heart was beating rapidly. She never liked being chosen for teams. She was often picked last.

Lucy said, "I am picking team leaders." Each leader would be asked to choose four students they wanted to be on their teams. The teams of five would then be given an assignment and sent out in the Overworld to complete it.

Julia watched as Nick, who was chosen as a team leader, chose his team. He picked Jamie, and he stared in Julia's direction as he chose the next person. As he completed his list of four people to be on his team, Julia was surprised he didn't call her name.

Lucy called the next team leader. "Cayla."

Julia smiled when Cayla called her name first, followed by Emma, Mia, and Brad. Brad wasn't happy about being chosen.

"I told you I don't like speaking in public," he whispered to Cayla.

"Please don't make us look bad. We have to work together," Cayla reminded him.

"Is everything okay?" Lucy asked.

"Yes," Brad replied. "I was just thanking Cayla for choosing me."

"Great," Lucy said and gave the group their mission. "Your group must go to the Nether and unearth the treasure from a Nether Fortress." She added, "There is a Nether Fortress that has many chests filled with valuable treasures. You must return to campus with gold horse armor, diamonds, and Nether wart. I want an extensive update on the entire trip when you return, which you will present in front of the school."

"Do we have a time limit?" Emma asked.

Lucy replied, "Whoever comes back first will be given priority, but as I said, this isn't purely a race. This is about working together and using your minds to solve problems skillfully. I don't want you rushing because it will just lead to sloppy work."

As Lucy gave the final instructions for each group, she wished them well. Julia was annoyed that many other groups were given challenges that took place in areas of the Overworld where she felt comfortable, including the Cold Biome. Julia's heart sank. She was fearful of the Nether. Her mind raced with images of wither skeletons and magma cubes. She didn't realize that her friends had already started crafting the portal to the Nether.

"Aren't you going to help them?" Lucy asked.

Julia apologized as she pulled obsidian from her inventory and took a deep breath.

Chapter 4
NETHER MEANT TO HURT YOU

The purple mist blurred Julia's vision, and she couldn't the see the sea of blazes and ghasts that flew toward them when they spawned in the middle of the hot, steamy Nether.

"Watch out!" Cayla screamed.

Julia turned around, narrowly avoiding falling into the lava stream behind her as she dodged the blast from the ghast.

"Don't hide from the fireballs," Emma called out. "Remember what I taught you. You have to use your fist."

Julia made a fist and struck the second fireball, which flew back toward the ghast, destroying it. She battled the ghasts with her fist, as Brad and Mia battled the blazes with their bows and arrows. When the final fiery flying mobs were destroyed, Julia let out a sigh of relief.

"I see a group in the distance," Brad said.

The group could see people sprinting toward what appeared to be a Nether fortress in the distance. Julia remarked, "It looks like Nick."

"And Jamie," Brad said.

"I don't know the other people he chose," Julia said.

"We have to catch up to them," Cayla said. "We don't want them getting to the loot before us."

Emma reminded them, "Lucy did say that she will give priority to the team that gets there first."

"But she also told us not to rush. I don't want to do a bad job," Mia said.

"I think we have to stop talking and get to that fortress," said Cayla as she sprinted past an orange lava waterfall on the netherack ground.

"Slow down," Julia begged. Cayla was way ahead of the group and they couldn't catch up.

"Not again," Brad called out.

Four ghasts flew toward them. The white blocky mobs lowered their tentacle-like legs and spit fireballs at the group.

Julia didn't need anyone to remind her this time that her fists were her best weapons. She swung her fist until she annihilated a ghast, picking up a tear that it dropped on the ground.

Cayla screamed, "Help!"

Julia could see Cayla surrounded by Nick and his group as she battled a ghast.

"Leave her alone!" Mia called out as she slammed her fist into a fireball, which boomeranged back toward the white floating blockhead and destroyed it. "Got some gunpowder," Mia announced as she picked up the dropped gunpowder.

Once the final ghast was destroyed, Julia sprinted toward the entrance of the Nether fortress.

"Leave her alone, Nick," Julia called out, but was shocked at the response. Nick called out for help.

As they sprinted toward the fortress, Julia could see someone standing by the entrance. "Oh my!"

Hallie stood in the entrance of the Nether fortress. Her blue hair was secured with her signature daisy hair clip, and her knee-high socks were uneven. "I escaped."

Julia wondered if this was a part of Lucy's plan, but she knew that Lucy would have never let Hallie out of the bedrock prison.

Hallie held a sword against Nick's unarmored chest. "Seriously?" She laughed as she asked Nick, "You traveled to the Nether without wearing armor? Your team should lose because of that one fact. I mean, how can you expect to survive here or anywhere without armor?"

Nick didn't answer. He just looked at Hallie as his hands shook.

"Do you think you're really going to get into this Nether fortress?" she asked.

"Hallie," Julia confronted her old roommate. "What do you want from us? Haven't you caused enough damage to the Overworld and Minecrafters Academy? Why did you have to escape from prison and bother us again? Haven't you learned your lesson?"

"Wow." Hallie laughed. "You have a lot of questions."

"And it seems you like you don't have a lot of answers," Julia said.

"I don't like your attitude." Hallie pushed Nick aside and lunged at Julia, repeatedly striking her with a diamond sword until Julia awoke in her bed at Minecrafters Academy.

"Mia! Emma!" Julia groggily called out to her roommates, but there was nobody there.

Julia sprinted out of the dorms, calling out Lucy's name through the empty campus.

Lucy sprinted from the great hall. "Is everything okay?'

Julia led Lucy toward the bedrock prison and walked Lucy into an empty cell. "Hallie has escaped."

Chapter 5
FIERY FRIENDSHIP

"**H**ow?" Lucy asked as they stood in the empty prison cell. "It's impossible to escape from here!"

"She's in the Nether. It's awful." Julia explained what happened in front of the Nether fortress and how she was destroyed by Hallie's diamond sword.

"We have to go there right now," Lucy said as she grabbed obsidian from her inventory and started to craft a portal to the Nether. Julia quickly gathered all of the supplies she had in order to help Lucy with the portal, then waited to be blinded by the purple mist.

"Where are they?" Lucy asked as they emerged in the Nether and thankfully weren't met by any hostile mobs.

"We have to find the Nether fortress," Julia said as she sprinted in the direction of the fortress. Lucy trailed behind her.

"It's right past this waterfall," Julia said, but stopped when she didn't see the Nether fortress. "Wait, this is where it was before. How could it be gone?"

"Are you sure you are in the right place?" Lucy asked.

Julia scanned the area. She recalled passing a lush lava waterfall as she reached the Nether fortress, but it wasn't there. "I'm not sure. I thought I did. I'm sorry."

A flock of blazes flew toward them, shooting flaming balls at them. Armed with their bows and arrows, the duo aimed at the blazes, destroying them one by one and picking up the dropped blaze rods.

Julia heard a voice. "Did you hear that?" she asked Lucy.

"Yes," Lucy stood still. "It sounds like it's coming from that direction," she said. They climbed up a netherrack platform, spotting the Nether fortress in the distance. Nick and Hallie were in the middle of a sword fight. Julia and Lucy climbed down from the platform, sprinting past lava falls, and running along a lava stream until they reached the fortress.

Julia splashed a potion of Weakness on Hallie, who laughed and shrugged off the potion.

"You're going back to prison," Lucy shouted.

"No, I'm not." Hallie slammed her sword into Lucy's arm. The group rushed toward Hallie with their weapons, striking her with swords, arrows, and potions until she was destroyed.

Lucy said, "I have to see if she respawned on campus. Please finish your assignment." She teleported back to Minecrafters Academy.

"That was crazy," Julia sighed. "I can't believe Hallie escaped."

"Do you think that was a part of our test?" Mia asked.

"That would be a crazy test," Julia said, "but I don't think so. Lucy seemed very upset that Hallie had escaped."

Nick asked both groups, "Should we work together to get the treasures from this Nether fortress?"

"If it helps us to win," Mia said.

"I'm not sure it will help us win, but I know if we don't work together, we'll lose," Jamie theorized.

The group entered the Nether fortress and made note of the items they needed to obtain while they were there.

"We need Nether wart," Julia said as she picked some from a patch that was growing next to soul sand at the side of the staircase.

"I see a chest," Brad called out.

Boing! Splat! Boing! Bounce! Splat!

"What's that?" Julia's voice quivered.

"Magma cubes!" Mia shouted as bouncy blocks filled the small dark room in the Nether fortress.

Julia's heart raced. Crimson blocks with orange and yellow eyes hopped toward them, and Julia cried, "I'm surrounded! Help!

"Use your sword," Emma called out to Julia. Emma fearlessly slayed the magma cubes. As she swung her sword into the gelatinous cubes they broke into smaller cubes, which Emma quickly destroyed with a couple of strikes from her diamond sword. Everyone followed Emma's lead as they worked to destroy the cubes, which dropped magma cream when they were destroyed.

"We've almost got them all," Cayla said optimistically.

As the final magma cube was destroyed, two black wither skeletons spawned and swung their swords at the group.

"We're never going to get the treasure," Mia sighed as she sprinted toward a wither skeleton, but the Nether-dwelling skeleton struck Mia and she was destroyed.

"Mia!" Julia called out. "Oh no! I hope this doesn't stop us from being chosen as class speaker."

Lucy walked into the Nether fortress as Julia spit out those words. "That's not the type of comment I'd expect from you, Julia."

Julia was stunned by Lucy's appearance, and the wither skeleton sensed her vulnerability and struck Julia until she disappeared.

Chapter 6
TREASURE HUNTERS

"**W**e lost," Julia called out as she respawned in her bed.

"Is it my fault?" asked Mia, who was standing in the middle of the room, getting ready to teleport back to the Nether.

"No, it was my fault," Julia confessed. "I said something I shouldn't have and Lucy heard it. It was awful. When you were destroyed, I didn't worry about you being destroyed. I was just worried about how you respawning on the campus would affect the group."

"That's not that bad," Mia said. "I actually thought the same thing."

"Thanks for making me feel better," Julia said.

"We have to get back to the Nether," Mia said. "We have to teleport."

Julia and Mia teleported into the Nether fortress, where Emma and Cayla were in the middle of battling three wither skeletons, and they joined their friends in the fight against the stone-carrying bony beasts of the Nether.

"They just keep spawning," Cayla cried.

"Where are the others?" Mia asked.

"Where's Lucy?" Julia asked.

Both Julia and Mia joined their friends in battle, striking the powerful wither skeletons.

"Lucy left with Nick's team," Cayla said breathlessly. "They have all of their treasures."

"What about Brad?" asked Julia as she destroyed a wither skeleton and leaned down to pick up the skull.

"I'm right here." Brad sprinted in carrying gold horse armor. "All we need are the diamonds. I think we can get them." Brad quickly placed the gold horse armor in his inventory and slammed his sword into the remaining wither skeleton and it was destroyed. He picked up the dropped skull.

"Let's get the diamonds," Julia said with a renewed energy. The group sprinted through the fortress, opening chests.

"I know there are diamonds in one of these chests," Cayla said. "Nick's group got them."

"Found them!" Mia called out from a room deep within the fortress.

The group sprinted toward Mia and gathered diamonds. Julia smiled. "It's time to go home."

Mia crafted a portal and this time the purple mist didn't bother Julia's eyes. She was happy to be out of the Nether with inventories filled with treasure.

Julia's mood changed when she realized they were the last team to return to the campus and everyone was waiting patiently for them. She knew that, at this point, they weren't top candidates for class speaker. Julia and her friends watched as each group made their presentation.

Brad whispered to his friends. "Please don't make me present anything. Can you guys do all of the talking?"

"Yes." Julia smiled.

When it was finally their turn, Julia was shocked when Lucy said, "I'm going to have to call out two teams that were confronted by a hostile force in the Nether. They worked together to get Hallie, a prisoner on campus, who has a history of terrorizing both the Overworld and Minecrafters Academy, back in her bedrock prison, where she won't be able to harm anyone."

Julia hoped this would keep them in the running, but she wasn't convinced. Since they had taken so long to return to Minecrafters Academy, by the time the group presented their treasures, the sun was starting to set.

As Mia explained how they worked together to gather the Nether wart, someone cried out, "An Enderman!"

An Enderman stared at one of the students and let out its usual high-pitched shriek as it teleported toward an innocent student.

"Run toward the lake," Julia called out to the girl, who seemed to be frozen in the crowd. Julia worried about the student and rushed toward her. "Run with me."

Julia and the girl with yellow hair sprinted together and jumped into the water. The Enderman trailed behind them and was instantly destroyed when it splashed into the deep blue water. Julia brushed the water out of her eyes as she swam back to shore.

Lucy regained order with the crowd, telling them to listen to the rest of the presentation, and reminding them that having respect for fellow students was a vital trait of a class speaker.

Mia continued to explain what had happened in the Nether, but the skies grew darker, and the sun was replaced with the moon, and soon the campus was under attack from a zombie army. With outstretched arms, the vacant-eyed zombies poured onto the great lawn, attacking anyone in sight. A foul smell of rotting flesh flavored the night air.

Julia quickly sipped a potion of Strength as she readied herself to battle the zombies that spawned in front of her. Splashing potions and using her sword, Julia was able to destroy a couple of zombies, but the new ones kept spawning, and Julia couldn't keep up.

"Help!" she cried. Although she didn't want to appear weak and vulnerable, she knew if she didn't call for help, she'd never survive.

Chapter 7
ZOMBIES

Mia and Emma were in the middle of their own battle as a cluster of zombies surrounded them, and they used everything in their arsenal to battle the vacant-eyed monsters.

"Help!" Julia screamed again as she slugged two zombies with her sword, weakening them, but not destroying the beasts.

Cayla came to Julia's rescue. She opened all her bottles of potion and splashed them on the undead creatures as Julia slammed her sword into them. "We got them!" Julia called out happily as they picked up an assortment of dropped items, including rotten flesh.

"The battle is far from over," Cayla said as she looked over at Brad, who was cornered by a group of vicious zombies. His health bar was incredibly low.

The duo sprinted toward Brad and struck the zombies with their swords, but it was too late, Brad was destroyed. Julia and Cayla continued to battle the zombies until Brad respawned and teleported to them.

"This battle is endless," Brad said as skeletons, Endermen, and other mobs of the night spawned throughout the campus. Zombies ripped doors from every building on campus, skeletons shot arrows, and the shrieks from the Endermen nearly deafened the students.

"Oh no!" Cayla cried as a spider jockey crawled toward them. "Not another spider jockey."

"It's okay. We're a team," Julia reassured her friend. "I'll focus on the skeleton and you can focus on the spider."

"What about me?" Brad asked.

"Just strike whatever you can," Julia said breathlessly. She traded in her sword for a bow and arrow and concentrated as she aimed at the bony beast, trying to knock it from the spider it was sitting on. Julia's first two arrows missed the skeleton and she was frustrated.

Brad shot an arrow, piercing the skeleton's arm and slightly weakening it. Julia followed with two arrows, which landed in the center of the skeleton, destroying it. Once the skeleton was gone, Cayla sprinted toward the spider and struck the red-eyed arachnoid until it was obliterated.

There was no time to rejoice as an Enderman locked eyes with Julia and let out a familiar shriek. Julia rushed toward the lake in the thick of the night. It was almost impossible to see and Julia wished she had a potion for Night Vision, but she was running low on potions. In fact, after these constant battles, Julia was running low on all supplies. The Enderman was right behind her, and Julia wasn't sure she'd make it to the water in time.

The Enderman reached out for Julia, but before it could inflict any damage, Julia jumped into the water. The cold water was refreshing, and she let out a sigh of relief as the Enderman dove into the water and to its watery demise.

"Are you okay?" Cayla called out.

Brad and Cayla stood on the shore, and Julia swam toward them. She'd unknowingly swam further than she wanted. The swim back to shore was long, and coupled with the frigid water and the cold night air, Julia was growing exhausted. She wanted to give up, but knew that if she did, there was no way her team would be in the running for class speaker.

Lucy raced around the campus, alerting students to return to the dorms and to safety. "Off the great lawn."

The students had done a good job of destroying the zombies and the campus was almost rid of the hostile mobs. Julia sprinted toward her dorm room, and was happy to find Mia and Emma in their beds.

"I'm getting tired of these night battles," Julia said as she crawled into bed.

Mia agreed. "I feel like we don't have time to learn, and we only have a few more weeks left at school. It's very upsetting."

"And finals start tomorrow," Emma reminded them.

Julia felt her stomach flutter. "Finals? Tomorrow? Are you sure?"

"Yes," Mia said. "Emma's right. I remember Henry talking about a final exam in his class. We'd better get to sleep. We need to be prepared for finals."

The roommates were drifting off to sleep underneath their comfy wool blankets when Lucy appeared at their door. Henry and Max stood alongside her.

"I'm sorry to bother you, but we just got news that Hallie has escaped again," Lucy informed them.

"What? How?" Julia sat up in her bed.

"I guess you haven't seen her," Henry said. "We thought she might come here first."

"Why?" Emma asked.

"Since you were the ones who spotted her in the Nether, we thought she might come here. She might blame you for getting caught and being placed back in prison," Max said.

"How does she keep escaping?" Emma asked.

"We're not sure," Lucy admitted, "but once we get her back in prison, we'll have a guard placed outside her door."

Julia was upset they hadn't done that already. She didn't want to get involved with helping them find Hallie. She had to get to sleep. She had finals in the morning.

A loud explosion rattled the campus. Julia sighed. She knew this was going to be a long night.

Chapter 8
FINALS AND FINALISTS

The hunt for Hallie wasn't as long as Julia expected. Aaron raced into the room, announcing Hallie had been found placing TNT around the dining hall. He'd stopped her before she destroyed the building, but there was a small explosion.

Julia asked, "Do you need me to rebuild the dining hall?"

"Thanks for offering," Aaron said, "but we have taken care of that. You guys should get rest. Tomorrow is the start of finals. I have a challenging alchemy final prepared for everyone."

Even after they left the room, Julia wasn't sure she could get to sleep. With the thought of Hallie's constant escapes and her upcoming final exams swirling around her head, she was wide awake. She took a deep breath and tried to fall asleep, but it was pointless. She'd be a wreck for the finals.

* * * *

Julia didn't remember falling asleep, but she awoke in the morning as the morning sunlight shined through their window.

"We have to eat a good breakfast before finals," Emma said as she stood by the window.

"Wow, you're already up." Julia climbed out of bed.

"Yes, I'm nervous about finals. I had a hard time sleeping," Emma confessed.

"Me too," Mia said as she got out of bed.

"Same here," Julia said. "I don't feel ready to take a final exam."

The girls woke up as they walked across the great lawn to the dining hall. Julia assessed the damage of the previous night's battle. Doors were ripped from their hinges, and there was a small mark on the side of the dining hall Hallie had tried to blow up.

"I bet Hallie escaped when a zombie ripped the door off of the prison," Julia remarked.

"I bet you're right," Mia said, "but we can't focus on Hallie. We have to prepare for our first final exam."

"We have Henry's final first, right?" Mia confirmed.

"Yes," Julia said. "A final on survival skills. We should all be experts on survival after these battles," she added as they entered the dining hall.

Julia and her friends filled up on food to regain their energy for the final exam. Brad joined them at their table. "We need to eat well. Today is the start of finals."

"Don't remind us," Emma said.

"I think we have to get to our first final now." Julia tracked the time and the gang took their last bites before their first exam.

There was not a sound uttered in Henry's class as he announced the final exam. The only sound that might have been heard was rapidly beating heartbeats from the crowd of nervous students. Julia regretted eating a large breakfast because her stomach hurt.

"I am about to spawn an Ender Dragon on campus. We will all go out to the great lawn and I will evaluate how you destroy this powerful winged beast," Henry explained.

The group followed Henry onto the great lawn, and waited for him to spawn the dragon.

The dragon's muscular wings flapped as it flew across the campus, unleashing clouds of purple smoke from its mouth as it roared.

Julia hid behind a large oak tree and aimed her arrow at the dragon, striking the side of the beast. The dragon roared, and a few students cowered in the corner. Others dropped their weapons. Many of the students in Henry's survival class had never encountered the Ender Dragon before and the powerful beast from the End intimidated them.

The Ender Dragon flew toward a group of students that stood by the entrance to the main hall. They leapt at the dragon with their swords. The powerful beast destroyed one of the students.

"Oh no!" Julia cried out.

The remaining students shot arrows, splashed potions on the beast, and tried to strike the flying menace with their swords. After their many strikes, the dragon was weakened, but it hadn't been destroyed.

Cayla sprinted toward the dragon, striking it with her sword. As it lunged at her, she sprinted back into the classroom.

Julia had the perfect spot to attack the dragon. Every time it flew past her, she hit the beast with her arrow, infuriating the Ender Dragon. It roared and flew toward Julie, but she hid behind the bark.

Brad slammed his sword into the belly of the dragon, leaving the dragon with only one heart. Julia wanted to aim her arrow and deliver the final blow, but Jamie sprinted toward the Ender Dragon, fearlessly leaping at the dragon and piercing the beast's flesh. With this last strike, the Ender Dragon disappeared, leaving behind a dragon egg and creating a portal to the End.

Julia stared at the portal, trying to avoid going anywhere near it. She didn't want to wind up in that hostile world.

Henry picked up the dragon egg. He thanked the class and told them he'd post the results soon. Julia was happy with her survival skills, and hoped she got a good grade, but she knew she could have fought harder. However, she hadn't wanted to dominate the battle. There were other students in the class, and everyone had to show Henry what they had learned. Despite having found an ideal spot to fight the Ender Dragon, which worked to her advantage, she knew she had to give others a chance to show off their own skills. Like the competition for the class speaker, it was always a challenge when working in a group.

"I'm so ready for lunch," Emma told her friends.

"Me too," Cayla said.

Before they could enter the dining hall, they were stopped when they heard Lucy call out, "Announcement."

Lucy walked around campus with a megaphone. She had an important announcement and everyone gathered on the lawn, ready to hear it.

"Do you think she picked the winner?" Julia asked.

"I bet she did," Emma said.

Lucy said, "I have chosen the finalists for the class speaker. I have chosen the members of Cayla's team."

Cheers went up, and Julia was thrilled that everyone supported her and her teammates. However, the joyous mood turned more serious when Lucy said, "Only one person from Cayla's team will earn the top honor of class speaker."

Julia looked over at her friends. She didn't like the idea of only one of them being chosen. Her heart raced. She felt sick. She wanted to drop out, but she knew it was too late.

"Team Cayla will travel to End City," announced Lucy.

The crowd was in awe. Many of them had never been to this dangerous city, and had only heard about it and the mobs that only lived in that world, and the treasures that could be found if you were daring or skilled enough to beat the Ender Dragon in his own habitat.

"Whoever comes back with the most treasures from End City will be the class speaker," Lucy said.

"When do we go?" Julia asked. Her heart beat so fast, she was sure everyone could hear it.

"Now," Lucy said.

Julia looked at her friends as they walked toward the End portal the dragon had created when he was destroyed. Julia felt like each step took a lifetime to take. Time seemed to slow down, and as she approached the portal, she tried to hold back the tears.

Chapter 9
LET'S START AT THE END

"Good luck!" voices called out as they all crowded onto the End portal.

"I've never been to the End," Cayla confessed.

"Me either," Brad said.

"I haven't been there either," Julia said.

Emma and Mia also had never traveled to the End. Emma said, "So this is a first for all of us. I guess this means we don't have an advantage over each other when we're there, since now we are competing with each other."

"I don't want to compete. I don't want to go to the End," Julia said as they stood on the portal and everyone said their goodbyes. "Stop!" Julia called out.

Lucy walked over to the portal. "Is everything okay?"

"No." Julia hopped off the portal. "I don't want to go to the End. I want to give up my spot on this team."

"Why?" Lucy asked.

"I don't want to go to the End. I've heard it's a challenging place, dark and creepy. I don't want to battle shulkers in End City. I'm happy staying here."

Julia wanted to add that she was also happy to stay at Minecrafters Academy forever, and all of this change was overwhelming her, and she wanted everything to stay the same. Instead, she protested her trip to the End.

Lucy reassured Julia. "The worst thing that could happen is you're destroyed and respawn in your room. I think, and I'm sure you'll agree with me, that not trying would be worse than trying and failing."

Julia wasn't sure she agreed with Lucy. There were lots of things she was glad she hadn't tried.

Cayla stepped off the portal. "You have to come with us, Julia. We're a team."

Emma followed and hopped off the portal. "If you really want to experience the world of Minecraft, you have to visit the End."

"I'm not sure I want to experience the world." Tears streamed down Julia's face.

Mia walked over to Julia. "If you don't go, I'm not going."

"Yes," Cayla agreed. "If we don't go together, we will just give another team a chance."

"Pick another team," some students began to shout and soon she heard a chant.

"New team. New team. New team . . ."

Julia was overwhelmed and felt as if she was going to faint. She tried to speak but nothing came out. She looked at her friends and wanted to apologize, but she just stared at them.

"You need to make a decision now," Lucy informed her.

Henry told all of the students to calm down. "Silence. Let Julia speak."

Everyone stared at Julia, but she didn't say anything.

"Can't you see she doesn't want to go?" Jaime screamed.

"You're forfeiting your chance if you don't say anything," Nick added.

"Julia, what are you doing?" Cayla was annoyed.

"This isn't fair." Emma's voice quivered as she spoke.

"You're going to make us all give up our chances!" Mia shouted.

Again, Julia just listened to her friends, but she didn't say anything. She felt terrible. She wanted to walk onto the portal to the End and just go, but every time she stared at the portal, her heart pounded.

Brad was the last to hop off the portal, "Julia, we really worked hard for this, and I know you're scared, but Lucy is right. You have to try. You can't let fear get in your way. Maybe you'll win, maybe you'll lose, but you have to try."

Everyone stared at Brad as he spoke, and as he realized it, his voice grew shakier. Julia saw it wasn't easy for Brad to stand in front of the entire school and persuade her to travel to the End. By helping Julia, Brad was able to conquer one of his biggest fears.

Julia didn't say anything about Brad's accomplishment; she simply stared at him and smiled. "Thanks," she said softly. "I'm sorry for causing a scene. I will travel to the End with my team. Thank you again." Julia walked toward the portal.

The crowd was upset. Some of them wanted a new team to be chosen. Lucy tried to control the shouting. "Everyone, please wish them well on their journey to the End. I know everyone here wanted to be chosen, and I understand how you feel, but we have to accept the results."

Jamie was the first to call out, "Good luck, guys."

Nick said, "It's going to be okay, Julia. You're going to do a great job, I know it."

The students cheered as the gang stood on the portal. Lucy smiled and wished them a good journey to the End.

Everyone huddled together and took a collective deep breath when they activated the portal to the End. When they were about to fade into the End, Julia could hear someone call out.

"Hallie! Hallie is missing again!"

"What? How?" Lucy screamed.

Julia wanted to jump off the portal and help Lucy and the others find Hallie, but it was too late. There was no turning back. In seconds, she'd be in the End.

Chapter 10
THE WINGED BEAST

A flash of blue sprinted by and Julia gasped. "It's Hallie!"

"Where?" Brad stood on the obsidian platform and scanned the area.

"I don't see her." Mia looked in every direction.

"I think you're just imagining things because you're nervous." Emma also looked around the hostile world, but didn't see anything.

Julia was so nervous her eyes could have been playing tricks on her. In any case, she didn't have too much time to think because the instant they stepped into the End, they were confronted by the Ender Dragon.

Cayla screamed, "Watch out!"

The Ender Dragon swooped down and emitted a cloud of purple smoke as it roared at the group.

Julia reached for her bow and arrow, but she fumbled. She could feel something gnawing at her feet. "Endermites!"

"Use your swords," Emma instructed.

The group slugged the endermites with swords while they tried to shield themselves from the Ender Dragon by hiding behind a pillar.

The Ender Dragon was relentless in the attack. Brad was the first to lose a heart from the Ender Dragon. Julia looked up from the pool of endermites that surrounded her feet and raced toward Brad.

"Drink this." She handed Brad milk.

As Brad sipped the milk, Julia traded in her sword for bow and arrow. She was pleased with her first strike, which tore into the dragon's wing. The dragon roared and flew toward Julia. Using the pillar as a shield, Julia ordered her friends to strike the dragon with their swords. The gang repeatedly struck the dragon until it was weak, but the beast simply flew toward the Ender crystals, instantly replenishing its energy levels.

"We have to destroy the crystals!" Brad hollered, but there was no time for strategies when they could barely survive in this inhospitable dimension. An army of block-carrying Endermen marched toward them, endermites swarmed at their feet, and the Ender Dragon was working at full energy. Arrows shot through the air at the Ender Dragon and the gang struck the Endermen and endermites with their swords, but they were overwhelmed by the battle. It took every weapon in their arsenal and every ounce of energy to not lose the battle.

Julia focused on the Ender Dragon, which she felt was the biggest enemy. If you didn't destroy the Ender Dragon, you'd never survive in the biome, and they'd never make it to End City. She stood behind the pillar shooting a barrage of arrows at the winged predator, but without destroying the Ender crystals, she was engaging in a useless battle. Julia had to make a decision. She would have to decide whether to leave the security of standing behind the pillar, and be exposed as she sprinted toward the Ender crystals and aimed her arrow. She knew she had to move.

Julia took a deep breath and shot an arrow at the Ender Dragon, and raced toward the crystals.

A loud piercing shriek surprised her and before she could hit the Ender crystals, Julia was face to face with two Endermen. She struck them with her sword, but they grabbed her and she lost two hearts. Julia only had two more hearts left, and she didn't have the time to grab milk or a potion of Healing. She had to battle the Endermen that stood in front of her, with the Ender Dragon right behind her.

"Help!" She could barely get the word out as she slammed her sword into the two Endermen. Julia was shocked when they were destroyed. Julia quickly turned around and leapt at the Ender Dragon with her diamond sword, but the dragon struck her and she was left with one heart.

Julia raced toward the pillar. Once she was safely behind the pillar, she grabbed a potion from her inventory and took a sip. Her hearts were restored. Before she returned to battle, Julia saw something—or someone—sprint past.

"Hallie!" Julia screamed out.

There was no reply except for Emma, who screamed, "Julia, please. We need help. Hallie isn't here. Don't worry about it!"

"We have a bigger battle to fight," Mia reminded her.

Cayla was destroying the endermites as they crawled on the obsidian platform. "Shoot the crystals!"

Julia's heart raced as she sprinted toward the Ender crystals and aimed. With one shot, she destroyed one of the crystals.

Brad was in a one-man battle with the Ender Dragon, and he pierced the side of the dragon with his sword. Emma and Mia were surrounded by Endermen, and used their swords to survive in the middle of attacks from the lanky mob dwelling in the End.

Cayla got the endermite situation under control. "Just call me the exterminator," she joked, but nobody was listening. Everyone was engaging in their own personal war.

Julia sprinted through the Central Island in the End to destroy the other Ender crystals perched on a pillar. As she sprinted a familiar voice called out to her.

The Ender Dragon spotted Julia on the center of the obsidian platform, and flew toward her. Julia wasn't sure which was more of a threat, the Ender Dragon or Hallie.

Chapter 11
WATCH OUT FOR CRYSTALS

"I'll take care of her," another familiar voice called out. "Lucy!" Julia screamed. She was relieved that Lucy was in the End.

"I have help," Lucy said as Henry, Steve, Aaron, and Max sprinted toward her and leapt at Hallie.

Hallie was surrounded and outnumbered by the faculty from Minecrafters Academy. Julia couldn't watch Hallie's demise because she was facing an immediate threat from the Ender Dragon.

Julia could feel the purple mist from the Ender Dragon's breath sting her eyes and she closed them as she swung at the Ender Dragon. She missed the dragon and almost fell off the obsidian platform into the darkness of the End, but she regained her balance.

Cayla swung her sword at the Ender Dragon, diminishing its health, and called out to Julia, "Get the Ender crystals. It's our only hope."

Julia raced toward the pillar with the Ender crystals, but her eyes were still sore from the purple mist, compromising her aim, and she kept missing the Ender crystals. She sent arrow after arrow flying through the air, but she kept missing the crystals.

"I'm back!" Hallie screamed into Julia's ear, and Julia felt an agonizing shooting pain through her arm. Hallie had struck her with a sword and the pain radiating down her arm was intense. Despite the attack, Julia was surprised when her arrow finally struck the Ender crystals and destroyed them.

"I thought Lucy destroyed you," Julia said.

"She did, but I came back," Hallie replied and struck Julia again.

Julia turned around, ready to strike Hallie, but Hallie was too close to hit with an arrow. Julia grabbed one of her last potions from her inventory and splashed it on Hallie.

Hallie's hearts grew as she laughed "You splashed a potion of Healing on me!"

Julia's heart sank. She had used her last potion on Hallie.

The Ender Dragon flew toward them and struck Hallie and Julia. Both lost hearts, but the impact wasn't as lethal to the recently reenergized Hallie. Julia only had a few hearts left, and she knew she had to be cautious or she'd wind up in her bed at Minecrafters Academy.

Julia used the distraction from the Ender Dragon to quickly trade her bow and arrow for a sword. She struck the blue-haired Hallie until she disappeared from the End.

"Help!" Emma screamed.

Emma and Mia were still surrounded by Endermen, but the lanky mob seemed to increase the size of their army.

"I got one!" Mia beamed as she slayed the Endermen.

"But more keep appearing." Emma was terrified.

"Just keep fighting." Mia obliterated two more Endermen.

Three Endermen surrounded Emma and she didn't know which direction she should turn. She slammed her sword into one Enderman until it was destroyed, and she jumped back, trying to avoid being hit by the other two purple-eyed mobs.

"Pick up the Ender pearls!" Mia reminded Emma, "We need those to get onto the End ship."

"If we ever reach the End ship. This battle is impossible. We are just going to spawn in our beds," Emma said.

"We can do it," Mia said. "I know it."

"Okay, if you say so." Emma slammed her sword into a lanky Enderman, destroying it. She picked up the Ender pearl and placed it in her inventory.

Julia wanted to cover her ears as she entered a zone of high-pitched shrieks. As Endermen spawned at their feet, Julia could hear Brad and Cayla screaming as they were slowly losing their battle with the Ender Dragon. Cayla hollered Brad's name, and Julia knew he had been destroyed.

When Julia couldn't hear Cayla's screams, she knew that she was also destroyed. Julia knew she was next. There was no way she was going to survive this battle with an empty inventory. She held her sword tightly as she struck as many Endermen as she could, but the battle was pointless. Within seconds, Julia was in her bed at Minecrafters Academy and couldn't be further away from End City.

"Julia." Cayla and Brad stood above her bed.

"We have to go back to the End," Brad said.

Julia agreed, but quickly sprinted to her closet. "Just give me a second," she said as she filled up her inventory with potions she'd stored in her chest. As Julia replenished her supply, Lucy walked into the dorm room.

"I'm sorry you have to deal with Hallie during your battle in the End," Lucy apologized.

"It's very upsetting. It's hard enough battling the Ender Dragon," Cayla admitted.

"We agree," Lucy said, "and we understand that this is an additional challenge."

"We will take this into account as we grade you for this battle," Max said.

"Grade us?" Cayla asked.

"Yes, you will be missing finals week, so this will count as your final grade," Lucy explained.

"Really?" Julia finished replenishing her inventory with supplies. She was conflicted about this new piece of information. Although she was relieved to miss her finals, she didn't want to be graded on this failing battle. Before

Julia could discuss her issues with this idea, the group was jarred to hear a noise in the hallway.

A laugh echoed through Julia's room. Everyone turned around to see Hallie standing in the doorway. Her dress was covered in diamond armor and one of her knee-high socks was bunched up at her foot.

"Miss me?" she asked as she leapt at Lucy with her diamond sword.

"What do you want from us?" Julia asked as she splashed a potion of Harming on Hallie.

"This time you actually got it right," Hallie snickered, despite losing energy from the potion.

"Leave us alone." Brad slammed his sword into her unarmored arm.

"I don't want to be in that bedrock prison anymore," Hallie screamed as she plunged her sword into Julia's leg. "And I want the people who but me behind bars to pay for their crimes."

"Crimes? You're the one who committed a crime." Julia couldn't believe what she was hearing. How could Hallie think they had to pay for her crime?

Chapter 12
ARE WE ALONE?

"**Y**ou have to get back to the End," Lucy instructed Cayla, Brad, and Julia. "We will take care of Hallie."

"So long!" Hallie laughed. "I'll see you in the End."

"Don't threaten us!" Julia screamed as she and her friends left for the End.

They emerged in the middle of the End, on an island. It was pitch dark and they couldn't find their friends.

"Emma!" Julia called out.

"Mia!" Brad hollered.

There was no reply. Julia took out her compass, but it was broken. Brad looked over. "Your compass won't work here."

"Neither will a map," Cayla added.

"But they have to be here." Julia walked around the floating island and called out her friends' names.

"The End is a tricky place," Brad said.

"I know, but I just thought we'd find our friends." Julia was upset. "I don't even see the Ender Dragon."

"I'm kind of happy about that," Cayla confessed. "I don't see Endermen or endermites either."

"Where are we?" Brad questioned.

They were on an island made of End stone. "We must be on an outer island," Cayla said as she walked deeper into the End. "But I don't see anything."

They heard a faint roar in the distance."

"I don't think they were able to destroy the Ender Dragon. We have to find them," Julia said as she raced toward the sound of the Ender Dragon's roar.

She heard a laugh in the darkness. Julia stopped.

"Why are you stopping? We have to keep going!" Brad called out.

"I thought I heard something. It sounded like Hallie's laugh," Julia said.

"Lucy told us that we shouldn't bother with Hallie," Cayla reminded her.

"This counts for our final grade," Brad said. "We have to go."

Julia followed her friends toward the sound of the dragon's roars and hoped they'd find their friends soon.

"Get ready to battle!" Brad called out as ten Endermen met them.

Julia grasped her sword and readied herself for battle.

"Just look down," Cayla said as she sprinted past the Endermen without making eye contact, and the block-carrying mob remained passive and didn't attack them.

Julia felt a few nips at her feet and she stomped on the endermites as she saw the Ender Dragon and her friends. Julia replaced the sword and picked up the bow and arrow. There were two Ender crystals atop the pillars and she knew if she didn't destroy those crystals, they'd never destroy the dragon and make it to End City.

Julia sprinted toward the pillars, but she was stopped when the Ender Dragon's wing struck her side and she almost fell back. She steadied herself, but the dragon lunged at her again, and she wasn't able to regain her balance.

"Help!" Julia cried.

Cayla sprinted toward Julia, slamming her sword into the dragon's side, but Cayla was also struck by the dragon and lost a heart. The gang crowded around the dragon, piercing the beast with their swords, but the dragon flew toward the crystals and replenished its energy.

Julia sipped a potion of Healing as she aimed at the Ender crystals, destroying one perched high atop a pillar. She only had one more Ender crystal to destroy when she heard laughter in her left ear. Julia turned around to see Hallie. "What are you doing here? Leave us alone!"

"Never!" Hallie screamed, hitting Julia's left arm with a diamond sword. Before Julia could retaliate, Lucy spawned and skillfully obliterated Hallie with her diamond sword.

"Thanks," Julia said.

"Just get back to your battle," Lucy said.

Julia aimed at the last batch of Ender crystals and shot her arrow, destroying them. "Good job," Lucy called out before she disappeared.

Lucy wasn't there to see Cayla defeat the Ender Dragon with two strikes from her diamond sword.

The friends cheered when the dragon was destroyed. Emma exclaimed, "Wow! End City, here we come!"

"Too bad Lucy wasn't here to see you defeat the dragon," Brad said, "since this is a part of our finals."

"What?" Emma asked.

"Lucy told us this battle will replace our finals," Julia explained.

"Yes, obviously Lucy was here to see Julia destroy the final batch of Ender crystals. You're totally the teacher's pet," Cayla said.

"What?" Julia was upset by her friend's comment.

"You heard me," Cayla said.

"No, I don't think I did." Tears filled Julia's eyes. "Repeat it."

"It's no shock, but everyone thinks you're the teacher's pet," Cayla said.

"Really? Why?" Julia tried to hold back the tears.

"It just seems like you're always getting commended by Lucy. She was the one who asked you to help with Hallie," Cayla explained.

Julia yelled, "Stop! She doesn't commend me and the only reason she wanted me to help with Hallie is because I was Hallie's roommate and I had to deal with Hallie when she was trying to destroy Minecrafters Academy and the Overworld. You can ask Emma and Mia, because they were there. They remember when Lucy didn't even believe me and I had to prove that Hallie was the dangerous one. Lucy once thought I was to blame for all of the horrible attacks on the campus."

"She's right," Emma said. "Julia was in the middle of Hallie's attacks and she had to prove herself to Lucy. She isn't a teacher's pet."

"I don't think Julia's a teacher's pet," Mia said. "I think it was just bad timing that Lucy couldn't see you destroy the Ender Dragon, but we'll let her know about it when we give our report on the trip."

"The report." Sweat formed at Brad's brow. He was worried about the report. He had almost forgotten about that part, and now he assumed it was a part of their grade.

"Are you still worried about public speaking?" Julia asked.

"Yes," Brad replied.

"But you did such a good job convincing me to travel to the End, in front of the entire school," Julia reminded him.

Brad admitted, "That was very hard for me."

"I know." Julia smiled.

Cayla walked over to Julia. "I'm sorry, I know I must have come across as a really mean person, but I was just so annoyed that Lucy was there to see you destroy the crystals. Also, if you didn't destroy those crystals, I'd never have been able to destroy the Ender Dragon."

"We work well together and I don't think anyone is a favorite. We all have to complete this challenge," Julia said.

"Yes, we have to work together or we'll never finish this test," Mia said.

"This counts for our final grade," Brad said.

"We all did so well at Minecrafters Academy that it would be a shame if we get a bad grade because we start fighting with each other. We have to work together," Julia said.

"We have to work together, but remember, the person who comes up with the most loot wins," Emma reminded them.

"Does anybody want my loot?" Brad joked.

They laughed until they stopped, frozen in their tracks as they marveled at the purple End stone castle looming in the dark skies.

"We're here." Julia grinned.

Chapter 13
HELLO, END CITY

"It's incredible." Julia eyed the large castle lit by End rods. The purple stone buildings weren't shaded in the dark.

"We should try to find an End ship. That's where we'll find the loot," said Brad.

A banner waved from the top of a large structure standing next to the castle, but Julia didn't feel a breeze as she scanned the landscape of this city deep in the End. "I don't see an End ship anywhere."

"We have to explore the city," Emma said.

"I think there's loot in the castle. Let's go there first," Mia suggested.

The group walked toward the massive castle, but stopped when Brad cried out in pain.

Everyone looked for an attacker, but they couldn't find anyone. Julia wondered, "Do you think it's Hallie and she's invisible?"

"I'm not sure." Brad looked around the city. "I can't find anything."

"It has to be Hallie," Julia insisted and held her diamond sword in her hand, pointing it at an imaginary invisible person.

"Julia," Emma said, "calm down. If it's Hallie, I think the faculty has it covered."

Julia knew Emma was right, but she was fixated on Hallie attacking them again. She was also annoyed that Hallie was damaging their final grade and their last few weeks at Minecrafters Academy. They had to concentrate on the challenge and not focus on being attacked by an escaped prisoner who had one goal, which was to destroy the Overworld. Yet there wasn't an answer for this attack.

"Ouch!" Brad cried out.

"What hit you?" Julia asked.

"Did you see anything?" Mia asked.

"No." Brad was dumbfounded. "I keep getting hit, but I have no idea where it's coming from."

The group walked toward the castle, until Mia cried, "I've been struck."

"Where?" Brad asked.

Mia held her leg. "Right here."

"We have to find out who or what is behind these attacks." Julia stood in front of the castle.

"I've lost four hearts," Mia said. "It couldn't be Hallie. She isn't that powerful."

"Do you see those white particles?" Julia noticed a white film near Mia's leg.

"Ugh! Ouch!" Emma wailed, as she grabbed her leg and began to float. "I'm levitating. What's going on? And I lost four hearts!"

"The closer we get to the castle, the more powerful these strikes are becoming. What are we going to do?" asked Julia.

"Let's go inside," Mia said.

Emma landed on the ground. "Really? That's your plan? I was just struck by something that made me levitate and you want to enter a building that most likely houses this enemy?"

"What else are we going to do?" Mia asked.

"Mia's right. We need to find treasure and the sooner we find it and fill our inventories, the sooner we can get out of here," Brad said.

Julia felt something strike her leg, and she began to float. "It's a shulker! I saw it. It's camouflaged in the bricks. It looks like a brick, but I saw it jump up and it had a yellow head."

"Where?" Mia asked.

"Over there!" Emma called out as the shulker peered out from a purpur block inside the castle's entrance. The shulker unleashed a series of pellets that struck them. The gang floated in the air for what seemed like an eternity as they tried to gather potions of Healing and milk from their inventories. They were all low on energy after losing multiple hearts from the attacks.

"We have to destroy the shulker," Julia said as she aimed her bow and arrow, but the shulker sheltered itself within the purpur block.

When Mia landed on the ground, she raced toward the shulker with her sword and slammed it into the block, but didn't damage it.

The shulker peered out, ready to attack the group, but Mia stuck the yellow-headed mob with her sword, weakening the beast. As Mia waited for the shulker to show its face again, Emma screamed out, "Oh no!" Mia turned around to see six shulkers approach them.

"It must have signaled to its friends that it was under attack," Mia said as she struck the purpur block, but it was pointless. The mob was snug in its armor.

Shulkers surrounding them in every direction struck the group. They were floating as they retaliated. Holding their bows and arrows tightly as they floated in the air, they were careful not to drop any of their weapons. The gang tried to shoot any shulkers that showed their faces.

"They're like turtles. They have shells to protect them. This battle isn't fair," Brad shouted.

"We have armor," Julia rationalized, but Brad was right. It was an impossible battle and they had to come up with a plan quickly because they had to enter the castle and get the loot and leave.

"Potion," Mia could barely spit out the word.

"What?" Julia said.

"Let's splash a potion of Invisibility of ourselves and then sprint into the castle," Mia said as she gulped a potion of Strength.

Julia shot a sea of arrows, destroying two shulkers. The victories made her confident they could win a battle over these boxy, tricky mobs. "Just keep shooting at the shulkers. I think we can defeat them."

Brad was struck again and wailed in pain as he struck another shulker with his arrow. "No, Mia's right. We should try the potion of Invisibility. I know we're destroying some of these creatures, but it's still a tough battle. We need to get into the castle fast. I want to get back to school."

"Let's meet inside the castle," Mia said as she gulped the potion.

The group sipped their potions, making them instantly invisible. The group sprinted into the castle, searching for treasure.

"We have to find the loot room," Brad breathlessly said as they sprinted through the castle, looking for treasure and yelling out to their invisible teammates.

"I found the room," Mia called out, walking into a room with two chests.

The potion wore off and each person was visible as they crowded around the regular chest and the Ender chest.

"Open them," Julia said.

Mia quickly opened the chest. "It's empty." She raced to the Ender chest and opened it, only to reveal another empty chest. "Seriously?"

"It looks like we weren't the first people to enter this loot room," Brad said.

"Do you think Hallie took it?" Julia asked.

"I have no idea, but it doesn't matter who took it," Emma said. "It just matters that it's gone."

"We have to get out of here and find the End ship before we're attacked by shulkers," Mia said.

"Too late," Brad cried as he floated in the air.

Chapter 14
TRAITORS AND TREASURE

Shulkers surrounded them, popping out from their shells to unleash pellets that both forced the group to levitate and weakened them. Two shulkers struck Mia as she flew above the purpur block floor. She had lost too many hearts and grabbed a potion of Healing from her inventory. "This is my last bottle," she announced and quickly took a sip.

"I restocked my inventory," Julia reassured her. "You can have some of my potions."

The gang aimed their bows and arrows at the purple blocky mob, but they were virtually impossible to battle, since they were safe inside their purpur blocks. Julia was pleased when her arrow struck two shulkers, destroying the pesky mobs. She lowered to the ground and hid behind one of the chests to avoid getting struck by the mobs. If she covered her legs, she'd be fine. Julia struck another shulker as her friends crowded behind the chests, joining her in the battle.

"We have to get out of here," Brad said. "We're wasting our time."

"I agree," Mia said. "but I don't have any hearts left, and I'm afraid I'll get hit by one of their pellets."

Julia handed Mia a potion of Healing. "Once you finish this, we have to get going. This is a useless battle."

Mia gulped the contents of the bottle and Brad called out, "Let's go." The gang sprinted down the halls of the castle, heading toward the exit until Julia spotted a staircase.

"We should go down here," Julia called out.

"No way," Mia said.

"Julia's right. There could be a loot room down there," Cayla said.

"Ouch!" Brad grabbed his leg as a shulker jumped out of a purpur block.

Julia aimed and hit the shulker. "Bullseye."

"Wow, you're an expert fighter," Emma said.

"No, that's your skill. I'm just trying to get out of here," Julia said. "Follow me."

The gang sprinted down the hall. Emma was the first in the room. Its walls were covered in banners.

"What's this?" Brad asked as he eyed the floor for shulkers.

"I'm not sure," Mia said, "but it's not a loot room."

The gang ran through a series of rooms until they finally reached a loot room. The room, like the one they had seen before, had two chests. Mia sprinted to a chest and opened it. "Diamonds," she beamed.

Julia raced over to the Ender chest. Leaning down, she opened the black and green chest. "Wow! It's filled with enchanted iron boots."

Julia and Mia filled their inventories as the group stood with their mouths gaping open in horror. Julia looked up. "What's wrong?"

"Are you seriously taking all of the treasures?" Emma asked.

"That's not fair," Cayla said.

"You can have it all," Brad said, and Cayla and Emma shot him a dirty look and he added, "but I agree it's not fair. We all found the treasure. You were just the first to open it."

"But we found it and opened it first," Mia said defiantly, "I'm not giving it up."

Julia felt something on her back. She turned around to see Emma's cold diamond sword touching the small portion of her unarmored back. "What are you doing?"

Cayla stood with her sword aimed at Mia. "Share the treasure or we'll destroy both of you."

"How can you do this to us? We're your friends!" Mia said.

"Friends? Are you joking?" Cayla walked closer to Mia and rubbed the sword against Mia's arm.

"Friends don't steal treasure from their teammates." Emma pushed her sword against Julia's back.

Two shulkers entered the room, bombarding the group with pellets, and soon they were all in the air and incredibly weak.

Julia looked over at Mia and couldn't help herself. "Only one of us can bring back the treasure, and I'm the one who deserves it the most. If it wasn't for me, Mia, this shulker attack would have destroyed you. I'm the one who was kind enough to offer you the potion. I'm the strongest team player in the group, and I should be the class speaker."

"You don't sound like a team player to me," said Brad, "I thought being a part of a team meant working together."

"What is happening to you? You used to be nice," Mia said as she quickly replaced her diamond sword with a bow and arrow and aimed at the boxy shulker. White particles flew through the air as the group tried to avoid being struck by the shulkers.

Two pellets struck Mia and her health was deteriorating. Julia handed Mia another bottle of potion, but she refused it. Julia questioned her motives. "But you'll be destroyed."

"I'd rather be destroyed by a shulker than take a potion from you. I thought you were one of my best friends. We lived together for years at school, and I've never seen this side of you. You always say you hate competition, but you are beyond competitive. You're brutal."

The words stung Julia and hurt more than a shulker's pellet. At that moment, she realized that competition had turned her into another person.

Julia announced, "I just really want to be the class speaker. Please don't hate me. I have a plan."

Chapter 15
SHIP OF FOOLS

"It had better be good," Mia said as she shot an arrow at the shulker, destroying it.

"When we destroy these shulkers, I will evenly distribute my loot. When wc get back to school, we'll all have the same amount and then all of us will have to be class speakers," Julia said as she aimed and struck the final shulker.

"I don't think it will work, but we can give it a try," said Mia.

"I don't want any loot," Brad protested as they all raced through the purple halls of the castle and out of the building.

"You have to," Julia urged him. "You can't be afraid of speaking."

"Stop," Emma said as she pulled diamonds from her inventory and handed them to the group. "Now we all have the same amount."

Julia took the enchanted iron boots, giving a pair to everyone in the group. She looked over at Mia. "I'm sorry. I really am."

Mia placed all of the loot in her inventory. "Thanks, but I don't care if I'm chosen as the class speaker. I was more upset by your actions. I am going to forgive you, but you can't do something like that again. I know this is important to you, but I thought you knew friendship is a lot more valuable than being chosen as a class speaker."

"I do. That's why I came up with the idea of each of us having the same amount of loot," Julia said.

"It's fine," Brad said. "You did the right thing and so did Cayla."

Cayla shouted, "Guys! Look!"

Everyone watched Cayla sprint toward a pier. At the end of the pier was an incredibly rare End ship.

"We found one!" Mia beamed.

Emma picked an Ender crystal from her inventory and threw it at the ship, and the group entered the floating ship made of purpur bricks.

They climbed up the ladder on the deck and took in the view of End City. Julia said, "Wow, it's incredible."

"I'm glad our team was chosen to participate in this contest," Mia said as she marveled at the purple buildings and the city lit by End rods. Despite being such an inhospitable environment, it was stunning, and the group soaked in the beauty of End City.

"We should check out the cabins," Brad suggested.

"The ship isn't too big, so we should be able to find the loot really fast," Mia said.

"Look at that dragon head!" Cayla exclaimed.

A dragon head was on the bow of the ship. Julia said, "We have to get that dragon head. That's an impossible find."

"What are we going to do?" Mia asked. "There's only one dragon head."

"We can play rock, paper, scissors," Brad suggested.

"We can share it," Julia said. "We will bring it back to the school and use it to decorate the entrance to the dorms."

"That's a good idea," Mia said. "That way people will remember us and our battle in End City."

"Hopefully it will inspire other people to take a chance and visit End City," Julia said.

"How are we going to get it?" Emma asked.

The gang climbed down the ladder as Brad volunteered to get the dragon head. "It's a one-person job. That said, if you see that I'm about to fall, can you let me know?"

Brad sprinted toward the bow and slowly walked along the narrow bow. The dragon's head's red eyes glowed in the veil of darkness at the edge of the bow. Brad paused and Julia called out, "You can do it, Brad. I know it!"

Despite these words of encouragement, Brad was frozen on the bow. He looked down.

"Just look ahead," Mia said. "You're almost there."

Brad took a deep breath as he continued to walk on the narrow edge and carefully reached over and grabbed the dragon's head.

"Good job!" Mia exclaimed.

Brad placed the dragon head in his inventory, and he slowly watched each step he took, making sure he didn't fall as he made his way back to the safety of the upper deck.

Cayla said, "We should search for the treasure."

"Yes," Julia agreed. "I want to go home."

They walked inside the ship's interior, exploring the cabins. The first room was small and had a brewing station. Mia raced toward the brewing station. "Should I make a potion? I need a potion of Healing," Mia said.

Julia walked over to the brewing station. "There are two bottles here." She held up two potions of Healing that were sitting next to the brewing stand.

"I'd love potions," Emma said, "but I think you should brew something when we get home. I just want to get out of here."

"We have to find the treasure room," Brad said. "I hear the treasures on an End ship are incredibly valuable."

Mia said, "Let's remember when we find a treasure that we are sharing it."

"We will," Julia said as she searched for the treasure room.

"Found it!" Cayla called out.

Julia looked down at the obsidian floor and at the two chests. Next to the chest was an item frame, which held an Elytra.

"Watch out!" Brad screamed as shulker shot an arrow that pierced his leg and he began to float in the small room.

A shulker's pellet hit Julia's leg. She stood in front of the mob with her arrow and waited for it to open, slamming her sword into the fleshy face and destroying the annoying blockhead before it could unleash another round of pellets.

"The shulker guard is gone. Now we can get the loot," Brad said.

Mia leaned on the obsidian floor and opened one of the chests. The chest had gold ingots. Cayla opened the second chest, which contained enchanted diamond chest plates. "Wow, these are fantastic."

"I wonder if we get to keep this stuff or if we have to donate it to the school," Brad wondered aloud.

"I hope they let us keep it," Mia said as she looked at all of the treasures in her inventory.

"You're not keeping anything," a familiar voice called out.

The group looked up as Hallie stood in front of them, holding a bottle of potion and a diamond sword.

Chapter 16
HEADING HOME

"There's no way you're getting our treasure," Julia screamed as she fearlessly leapt at Hallie.

Hallie splashed the potion as Julia shielded herself from the potent drops, but they weren't aimed at her. Hallie poured the potion on herself and instantly wore a cloak of invisibility.

"Ouch!" Emma cried. "She struck me with her sword."

Mia couldn't fight back. Before she had a chance to grab her sword, Hallie slammed her sword into her and Mia disappeared.

Brad attempted to fight back, but every time he leapt at Hallie, it was just air. "I can't find her."

"But I found you!" Hallie hollered as she slayed Brad.

"Oh no," Julia was worried because there were only three of them left. Julia leapt at what she believed to be Hallie, and she pierced Hallie's body. Hallie was angered and used all of her energy to destroy Julia. The only thing Julia remembered from the battle was waking up in her bed in Minecrafters Academy.

Julia immediately sat up and looked through her inventory, and sighed with relief that all her items were still there.

"Julia," Emma called out from her bed. "What happened?"

"Hallie," Julia explained. "She destroyed us."

"We can't let her get away with this." Emma got up from the bed. "We have to stop her."

"It doesn't matter. We still have our stuff in the inventories. Hopefully everyone will spawn soon and we can go to Lucy."

As Julia spoke, Mia spawned in her bed. "What happened?"

"Hallie. That's what happened," Emma said.

"Check your inventory to see if you have everything," Julia said.

Emma searched through her inventory, confirming, "Yes, I have everything. We should go find Brad and Cayla."

The group didn't have to travel very far because Brad and Cayla sprinted into their rooms, but they weren't alone. Hallie stood behind them with her diamond sword pointed at their backs.

"What do you want from us?" hollered Julia, who raced toward Hallie with her sword and a potion of Weakness. She splashed the potion on Hallie, but Hallie dodged the liquid and it landed on Brad and Cayla.

Hallie laughed. "You harmed your friends. Good job."

"That was a mistake," Julia said as she struck Hallie with her sword. "But this isn't."

Hallie was irritated that Julia had depleted one of her hearts. "This is war." Hallie lunged at Julia.

Emma and Cayla shot arrows at the Hallie, weakening her. The effect of the potion of Harming was diminishing and Brad and Cayla gathered enough energy to grab their swords and join in the battle. Everyone was surprised when Lucy sprinted down the hall with Aaron, Max, Steve, and Henry.

Lucy shouted, "Don't destroy Hallie!"

The gang put their weapons down. Henry informed Hallie, "You're going back to prison. We don't need you terrorizing the campus anymore."

"There's no way you're going to force me back to that bedrock prison," Hallie shouted at the group.

"What do you want? Do you want to get out of prison?" Julia questioned her old roommate.

Hallie paused. "Yes, I want to get out of prison."

"Maybe Lucy will let you." Julia said.

"What are you talking about?" Hallie asked.

"I think the idea that you can never leave the bedrock prison is what is prompting you to escape all the time. If you knew you only had to stay there for a certain amount of time and then could prove that you were done terrorizing the Overworld, you might not dislike being in there so much," Julia explained.

Lucy nodded her head. "That's a smart idea, Julia."

Julia was worried that comment would make her friends think that she was a teacher's pet, but they didn't. Instead her friends complimented her on the good idea.

Hallie paused with her diamond sword pointed in their direction. "How do I know you're going to let me out?"

"If you stay there without incident, I promise to eventually let you back on campus, but we will keep a close eye on you," Lucy said.

Hallie made a rare confession. "I'm supposed to be graduating with you guys." She looked at Julia and her friends. "But instead I'm staying on campus."

Julia wanted to blurt out that she was jealous. She wished she could stay on campus, but she knew it was time to leave. She had been there a long time and learned what she needed to, and now she must return to the Cold Biome and continue her life as a builder.

Hallie said, "I'll go back to the bedrock prison, if I am given a time when I might be released."

"I guarantee it," Lucy said as she escorted Hallie back to her small bedrock room, where she would have a view of the graduation on the great lawn, but would not be able to participate with her fellow classmates.

Julia looked at her friends. "We did it. The battle with Hallie is over."

"And so is our trip to End City," Cayla said.

"But we never got the Elytra," Brad remarked.

"Next time," Julia said.

Henry said, "We have to meet with Lucy and count all of your loot."

Lucy spawned in the center of the dorm room. "Did someone say my name?"

"Yes," Henry said. "We have to count their loot."

"About that." Julia looked down as she spoke. She was afraid she'd get in trouble for changing the rules. "There's no need to count it. We don't have a winner."

"What?" Lucy appeared confused.

Brad explained, "We all have the same amount of loot. We found it together and divided it amongst us."

"Wow," Max exclaimed. "What a fair way of going about this test."

"Yes," Lucy said. "It's hard to work as a team and it's even harder to give up recognition for your individual work, but you guys have proved that you can work together. I guess I'll have to change the plan of having one class speaker."

"What?" Brad gasped. "No, you can pick one. Let's just find another way."

"No," Lucy said, "you all deserve to speak at the graduation."

"All of us?" Brad needed clarification.

"Yes," Lucy said. "Is there something wrong?"

"No," Brad said, "it's fine." His heart beat fast and sweat formed on his head.

Lucy suggested, "You should all write a speech together. Chose one word that describes your time at Minecrafters Academy and announce it at graduation instead of one speech."

"We just have to say one word?" Brad asked.

"I think I'd like you to pick one word and then explain why you chose it," Lucy said. "It can be any length."

Brad let out a sigh of relief, as Julia's heart began to beat rapidly. Her mind was blank. She couldn't think of any good words and graduation was just a couple of days away.

Chapter 17
THE SPEECH

"Is this yours?" Mia asked. She held a copper sword as she packed up the dorm room.

"No, I think it's Emma's sword," Julia replied as she paced the length of the room.

"Aren't you going to pack?" Mia looked at Julia's side of the room, which was filled with chests. She hadn't placed anything in her inventory.

"I can't pack. I'm still working on my speech," Julia said.

"Are you having a hard time coming up with a word to describe your experience at Minecrafters Academy?" Mia asked.

"No, I'm not having a hard time coming up with a word. The problem is that I have too many words and I can't narrow it down," Julia explained.

"Maybe I can help you," Mia stopped packing and stood at the edge of her bed and adjusted the wool blanket. "Why don't you read your list of words and I can help you narrow it down to one?"

"I can't read the list."

"Why?"

"I have more than three hundred words."

"Really? More than three hundred?"

"Yes." Julia paused. "Maybe I can read the top choices."

"That's a good idea."

"Engaging, productive, memorable, life-changing." She stopped and questioned, "Do you think life-changing is one word or two?"

"It would count as one."

Julia continued. "Incredible, monumental, friendship—"

Mia interrupted her. "A lot of these words mean the same thing. I think the best one so far is friendship. Obviously when someone comes to school they learn how to be productive or engage in a lesson, but one of the hardest things to learn is how to be a good friend. I know it sounds simple and basic, but it isn't."

"I know," Julia recalled. "Remember what happened in the End? I tried to keep all of the treasures."

"Yes, but you realized that it wasn't the right thing to do and we worked out the problem."

Julia reflected on their conversation. "You're right. I should write about friendship."

Mia walked toward the closet and continued packing, as Julia prepared to write the first draft of her speech. Her mind was racing. There were so many thoughts and she wasn't sure how she'd be able to put them all on paper. She wanted to write a memorable speech. As she thought about what she'd say, she watched Mia pack.

She was going to miss being a student at Minecrafters Academy.

Cayla, Brad, and Emma walked into the room. Cayla announced, "I finally finished my speech. It's about friendship."

"Friendship?" Julia's voice cracked.

"Yes," Cayla said. "Do you want to hear it?"

Julia explained that she was also working on a speech about friendship. "But it's okay because I haven't started it yet."

Julia left the room and took a walk around campus for inspiration. She passed the bedrock prison and saw Hallie staring out the window.

"Hey, Hallie." Julia peeked inside the prison.

Hallie smiled. She pushed her blue hair from her face and asked, "Did you come to visit me?"

"Yes, I wanted to say goodbye. Tomorrow is graduation," Julia said.

"You were chosen as class speaker, right?"

"A few of us were chosen."

"I can't wait to hear what you have to say." Hallie smiled.

As Julia walked away, she thought about Hallie and how things had changed between them. In her wildest dreams she'd never thought she'd have a conversation with Hallie, yet she just did. As she walked along the lake that framed the campus, Julia thought about how

Minecrafters Academy truly changed people. Yes, they left as as experts in their field, but there was another change that happened, one that was deeper than learning how to build or brew potions.

Julia knew what she was going to say at graduation and she was thrilled.

The next morning the campus was busy getting ready for the festivities. Brad looked up at the stage and began to panic. Julia walked over to him.

"Nobody is going to hear me because my heart will be beating so loudly that they won't hear my words." Brad's voice quavered as he spoke.

"You're going to do a great job," Julia said. "I know it."

"Maybe you should go first," Cayla suggested, "so you can get it out of the way."

Brad reluctantly agreed to go first, as Lucy called each of them up on the stage.

"These are the class speakers. They've also kindly donated the dragon head they retrieved from an End ship. It will sit at the doorway of the dorms," Lucy said as she looked in the direction of the majestic dragon head that was mounted outside the dormitory entrance.

Brad was the first to read his speech. He took a deep breath. "Headmistress Lucy told us to each choose one word that describes our time at Minecrafters Academy. My word is encouragement. I will confess that I am deathly afraid of public speaking, which I'm sure you can tell right now. I didn't want to stand up here, but the people I've met here encouraged me to do this and take chances. I'm glad I did. Whether it was public speaking or learning how to build something unfamiliar, like a house to grow mushrooms on the farm, I've learned a lot here and for that I will always be grateful. As I leave here, I'll remember that when I'm afraid to do something, it's often for the best that I try to do it. It's the only way to grow. Thanks, everyone, for helping me."

The crowd cheered.

Emma stood on the stage and read, "Mine is similar to Brad's, because the word I chose was courage. Also due to the encouragement from the faculty and my fellow students, I learned how to be brave and have the courage to take chances. I've always been a warrior and am prepared to battle. However, there was a period when I was afraid to battle. Everyone here taught me to have the courage to battle again. It wasn't easy and there were times when I froze in battle, but they wouldn't let me fall. If it weren't for you guys, I wouldn't be on this stage. Thanks."

The crowd clapped their hands as Cayla walked onto the stage. "I chose friendship. My friendships here are more valuable than any skill I learned here. There were times when our friendships were in jeopardy and we began to compete against everyone, but in the end, friendship overcame adversity. Thanks."

The students cheered, and they quieted down as Mia began to read. "I want to thank everyone for being chosen to speak. My word is teamwork. It was here that I learned how to be on a team, and what it really means to work together. Before I attended this school, I was working alone as an alchemist, selling my potions to travelers.

But here, I learned to work with others in competitions and classes. I actually thought I knew everything I had to before I started here, I really wondered what I could learn and what the people here could teach me. Once I met the faculty and saw Aaron's incredible brewing skills, I quickly understood there was a lot to learn. I also picked up other interests. Now, I am not only an alchemist but I'm a farmer. I never thought I'd be a farmer. Thanks for the experiences."

Julia was the final speaker. She took a deep breath as she waited for the students to stop cheering. "I had a hard time narrowing down the word I had to pick. In fact, I had more than three hundred words on my list. It wasn't easy to come up with one. This one might seem odd, but I picked growth. For the past few months, I couldn't stop focusing on the fact that school is ending. I love it here. I love it here so much that I really never want to leave. However, I realized while attending the school that the most important skill I learned was how to grow. My friendships transformed, my skills grew, and, most importantly, we all grew as people. I know leaving is going to be hard, but like everything, it's a part of growing. I'm glad I was able to attend this school. I'll miss everyone."

The cheers were deafening. Everyone was ready to celebrate at the graduation party.

Julia still wanted to stay at the school, but she knew there would be new adventures in the Overworld.

Chapter 18
THE GRADUATION

Jamie called Julia's name and said, "You did a great job with the speech. I think we're all having a hard time moving on. We're going to miss the school."

Cayla sprinted over to Julia. "Good news!"

"What?" Julia needed good news. Although this was a celebration, it was bittersweet.

"Emma and Mia had the best idea." Cayla smiled.

Emma and Mia raced over. Emma said, "Did she tell you?"

"Not yet." Julia couldn't wait to hear the good news.

Mia said, "We're planning a post-graduation trip. We're going on a treasure hunt in the jungle. You have to come."

"Really?" Julia was excited. She was going to miss her friends, but now she was able to spend extra time with them and go on an adventure.

"Can I join?" Jamie asked.

"Yes. The more, the merrier," Mia replied.

"We have to invite Brad," Julia said.

"Invite me where?" Brad walked over. He held a plate filled with cookies and offered them some.

"We're going on a treasure hunt in the jungle," Julia explained. "It is going to be a post-graduation trip."

"How long will it take?" Brad asked. "I actually have a job I must start."

"I do, too." Mia told them about the various farms she was hired to construct around the Overworld.

Emma said, "This isn't a very long adventure, but it will be fun."

"I'm in." Brad smiled and took a bite of his cookie.

Lucy walked over to the group. "I'm sad to see you leave, but I'm glad that you were able to attend the school. I'll always remember you guys."

"We'll always remember our time here," Julia said.

Aaron, Max, and Henry joined them. "I have your final grades," Henry announced.

"I hope we didn't fail. Then we'd have to stay here for another year," Julia joked.

"Everyone passed. I was impressed with your skills battling the Ender Dragon," Henry commended them. "I bet those skills came in handy when you were in the End."

"Yes, they did," Julia said, "but Cayla was the one who ultimately destroyed the Ender Dragon."

Cayla blushed. "I couldn't have done it if you hadn't destroyed the Ender crystals."

Lucy said, "I also want to congratulate you on completing your final exams. As you know, your trip to the End substituted for the remainder of your finals, and I'm happy to announce you all have earned an A."

Julia smiled at her friends as Lucy handed them their diplomas. She placed her own diploma in her inventory. After their post-graduation treasure hunt, when Julia was finally back at her igloo in the Cold Biome, she would put the diploma on her wall and think about her time at Minecrafters Academy and all the amazing adventures she'd had while attending the school. As she looked out at the great lawn filled with students celebrating at the graduation campus feast, she knew these years at Minecrafters Academy would be lifelong memories.

The End

READ ON FOR AN EXCITING SNEAK PEEK AT THE FIRST BOOK IN

Winter Morgan's Minetrapped Adventure

series

Available as a complete boxed set wherever books
are sold in September 2017
From Sky Pony Press

Chapter 1
AFTER SCHOOL

Simon had already gotten two warnings from his teacher about passing notes, but he couldn't help himself. He did want to learn about long division, but he also wanted to remind his friends Lily and Michael about the Minecraft game they had scheduled after school that day. Simon had spent the last few months playing with his friends on a multiplayer server where they had created a small town. Today they were going to finish a large roller coaster they were building outside of the village. Simon couldn't wait to test the roller coaster. He had to remind his friends about the meet up. When the teacher wasn't looking, he quickly tore a piece of paper from his notebook and ripped it in two. He wrote the same message on both sheets: "4 p.m. Today. Meet in the Overworld. Let's ride the coaster."

As Simon's teacher discussed a long division problem on the blackboard, he passed the first note to Lily, who sat next to him. She read it and nodded her head. Simon knew passing the second note was going to be a bit more complicated because Michael sat at another table. He looked over at Michael, who was busy trying to figure out the math problem on a piece of paper and didn't see Simon staring at him. Simon aimed and threw the note at Michael, but the teacher turned around and spotted the flying paper.

"What was that?" his teacher, Mrs. Sanders, asked, walking over to where the note had fallen on the floor. She picked it up and looked at the note, then asked, "Who wrote this?"

Simon's heart was racing. He sat silently and didn't raise his hand.

"Okay, I'm going to ask one more time. Who wrote this note?"

Again, nobody raised their hands.

"I told you guys, I don't like note passing. You have to pay attention to get the most out of your education." Mrs. Sanders lectured the class on the importance of long division.

Simon didn't want to admit that he wrote the note. He already had two warnings and he could feel Mrs. Sanders staring at him.

"The class is going to lose recess if someone doesn't admit to throwing this note," Mrs. Sanders announced.

Simon panicked. He knew he might get sent down to the principal's office if he admitted that he wrote the note. He didn't know what to do, so he did nothing.

"Nobody will admit to writing this note?" Mrs. Sanders held the paper up, walking around the classroom to show the kids the note. Her red nail-polished fingers clutched the small piece of paper.

"Everyone is losing recess. You get to spend the half hour you usually get to spend playing in the schoolyard, sitting in this class working on five long division math problems I'll write on the board."

The class let out a collective groan.

Melanie, who sat next to Lily, raised her hand. "I don't want to be a snitch, but I think I know who wrote it."

Mrs. Sanders said, "Melanie, I want the person who wrote it to admit they were passing notes." Mrs. Sanders looked at the note again. She knew it was about Minecraft.

Simon looked down at his black T-shirt with an image of a creeper on it. He could feel Mrs. Sanders staring at him. Simon didn't want Melanie outing him in front of the class or telling everyone that he was responsible for the class losing recess after school.

Simon raised his hand and admitted, "I wrote the note."

"Thank you for admitting that you wrote it." Mrs. Sanders looked at Simon, and then said to the class, "You will have recess. But Simon, you must stay behind. I need to talk to you."

Simon sighed. He could see Michael staring at him and whispering, "I'm sorry."

The class left for recess and Simon stayed in his seat. Mrs. Sanders called him over to her desk. "Simon, please come here."

Simon walked with his head down. He feared what Mrs. Sanders would say. He didn't want her to call his parents or send him to the principal.

"Simon, I know you love Minecraft and you're very excited to play the game with your friends after school, but you have to pay attention in class. Math is a vital skill. You might even need to use a bit of math in Minecraft."

Simon thought about the ways he used math in Minecraft. He did need it when he was building and creating servers. He nodded. He knew Mrs. Sanders was right.

"Do I have to go to the principal's office?" he asked.

"No, you can go outside and join the others at recess. I am not giving you another warning. I was impressed that you took responsibility and admitted you were wrong in front of the class. Although you made a bad decision in writing the note, it shows good character that you admitted your fault. But if this happens again, you will go to the principal's office."

Simon promised he would never pass another note in class, and left to join his friends in the schoolyard.

"Simon," Lily shouted across the schoolyard.

Michael and Lily rushed toward him. "What happened?" asked Michael.

"Nothing, really," he replied. "But that was pretty awful, wasn't it?"

"Yes," Lily agreed. "You can't pass notes anymore."

"If I had only caught it, everything would have been fine," Michael apologized.

"That's not the point," Lily remarked. "Simon shouldn't be passing notes at all."

"Agreed," Simon said. He quickly added, "I am so excited to ride the new coaster."

"Me too." Michael was talking about the most recent updates he had made to the ride when Melanie walked over to them.

"Didn't you learn the first two times you got in trouble? Passing notes isn't allowed in class," Melanie said matter-of-factly.

Simon had been avoiding Melanie since kindergarten, when she was labeled the class snitch. Now they were in fifth grade and she was still telling on people. "You should mind your own business, Melanie."

Melanie just shrugged and walked away.

Just then, the lunchroom monitor announced that everyone had to go inside for lunch. The gang walked into the lunchroom and got in line.

"I hope they have chocolate milk today," said Lily.

"How can you think about chocolate milk when we're going to test out the most extreme roller coaster in Minecraft? Man, everyone on our server is going to be jealous of us." Simon rattled on about the ride.

"I hope nobody destroyed it. You know how much I hate griefers," Lily remarked.

Simon's jaw dropped. It had never occurred to him that a griefer might destroy his coaster, but now it was all he could think about. He couldn't concentrate for the rest of the school day. He was too preoccupied with his roller coaster. He couldn't wait to get home and see if it was still functioning.

Chapter 2
LIGHTNING STRIKES

When the school day finally ended, Simon rushed home and turned on his computer. Lily and Michael weren't on the server yet. In the Minecraft world his name was HeroSi, Lily was QueenLil, and Michael was DiamondHunter. The group always stuck together and went on numerous treasure hunts.

HeroSi had a large house, on a farm where he grew potatoes and carrots. He also had a flock of sheep and an ocelot named Meow. Simon loved his Minecraft world. It was his escape from the real world, where Mrs. Sanders forced him to learn long division, and where his parents reminded him to do his chores. In fact, he knew he needed to take out the recycling right after he finished his Minecraft game. He was only allowed to play for one hour and then his screen time was over.

Simon was relieved to find the coaster still intact—nobody had destroyed it. With a smile, he began to add the finishing touches to the ride.

A message popped on the screen. His friends were on the server.

"Are you excited to test out the coaster?" asked Simon.

"Is it done?" Michael replied.

"Almost." Simon finished the last of the minecarts they would ride in. "Now it's done."

Simon, Lily, and Michael hopped into one minecart, cheering, "Let's go!"

The trio rode in the coaster. Simon let out a scream as his and his friends' characters went down the first big drop on screen, and he was glad his friends couldn't hear him.

The roller coaster climbed toward its second big drop and Simon couldn't wait until they reached the top.

"We're almost there," said Lily.

"I know! This rocks," added Michael.

"Whee!" Simon was thrilled as they reached the bottom of the biggest drop.

The ride was over. Simon could barely believe that they hadn't ridden an actual roller coaster. Although it was crafted on the computer, he had felt all the drops.

"Now that we've ridden it, we have to come up with a name. What should we name the coaster?" Lily loved naming everything. She had named their town, their houses, and all the pets. She had even named Simon's ocelot Meow.

"The Big Dipper?" suggested Michael.

"I think that one's been used. Let's make up something really cool," Lily said, and then followed it with a list of potential names. "The Flyer, Dropper—"

"Let's not worry about names right now," Michael said. "I just want to ride it again!"

"Okay," Lily replied, and they all hopped in the mine cart for another ride on the unnamed coaster.

Simon thought the coaster was better the second time around because he didn't have to worry if there were any glitches, and he knew he was in for a smooth ride.

"Again?" asked Simon. But before he could hop into the minecart for a third ride, his mother walked into their small home office, where they kept the family computer. "Simon, you have to get off the computer. There's been a tornado warning."

"A tornado?" Simon couldn't believe it. There were never severe storms in his part of the country. "Are you sure?"

"Yes, the news is warning everyone. We have to get to a safe spot in the house. Your brother is already in the basement. Come quickly." Her voice shook, and she sounded very nervous.

"Guys, did you hear there is a tornado warning?" Simon asked Michael and Lily.

"What? How do you know?" Michael hadn't heard about the warning.

"My mom just told me. I have to shut off the computer and go to the basement."

"My dad just told me that we have to go to the basement, too," Lily said, just as they all heard the crash of thunder in the distance.

"Wait. Do you see that person near the coaster?" Michael asked them.

Simon looked at his computer screen. There was a person dressed in a green jumpsuit walking toward the coaster. He was carrying what looked like a brick of TNT.

"We can't leave. That looks like a griefer," Lily remarked. "But my dad is really upset. He says we have to get to the basement as fast as we can because the storm is approaching."

Simon could hear his mother shout his name from the basement. "Where are you? This isn't a joke! You could get seriously hurt."

Simon knew his mom was right, but there was someone about to blow their coaster up. They had worked on that roller coaster for three months. He didn't know what to do.

"Michael, Lily. Are you still there?" he asked.

"Yes," they both replied.

"We have to stop this griefer now." Simon grabbed his diamond sword and dashed toward the person in the green jumpsuit.

Michael and Lily joined their friend. As the trio leapt at the griefer, he grabbed a bottle from his inventory and splashed a potion of weakness on the gang. They grew frail, but they still had enough energy to strike the griefer with their diamond swords.

"He's not alone," Michael spotted another person in a green jumpsuit carrying bricks of TNT.

Lily used her last bit of energy to move toward the other griefer. She lunged at him, destroying the griefer with her diamond sword.

"Good job," Simon told Lily as she ran back to help her friends battle the stronger griefer.

"Simon!" His mother hollered from the basement, "Get down here!"

The sound of thunder boomed through the house again. "Did you hear that, guys?" Simon asked his friends.

"It sounds like a TNT explosion, but it's coming from the real world," Lily wrote. "My dad is calling me."

"I got him." Michael was lost in the game, not paying attention to the storm. He struck the griefer and destroyed him.

"Simon!" His mother sounded frantic, her voice halfway drowned out by another peal of thunder. The lights and the computer screen flickered as lightning lit up the sky.

Simon made to shut the game down, already reaching for the computer's power button, when a lightning bolt struck the house and the lights went out completely. He fell to the ground. That was the last thing he remembered.